A Day in School
The Kid Goes on Vacation
The Kid Got Lost in the Zoo

Written and Illustrated by

JAN ALEXANDER QUINTOS

To order additional copies of this book, contact:
Xlibris
1-888-795-4274
www.Xlibris.com
Orders@Xlibris.com

A day in School

One morning, a kid wakes up.

He brushes his teeth then goes downstairs.

He eats breakfast and
takes his vitamins.

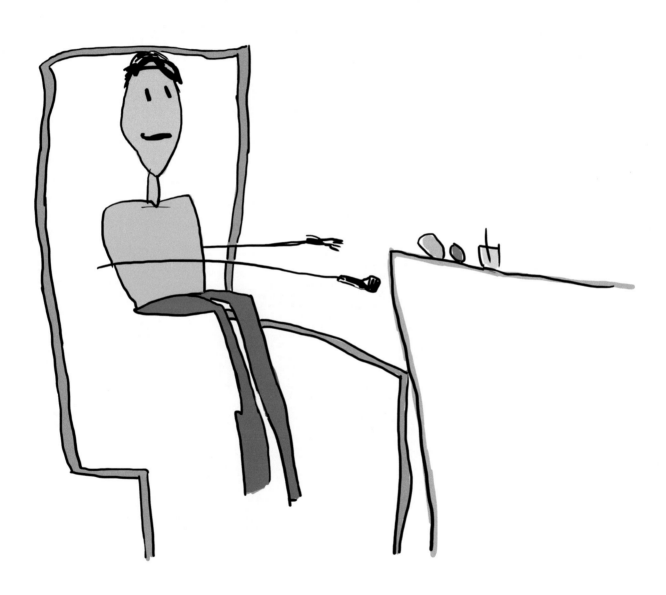

He changes his clothes, puts his shoes and socks on.

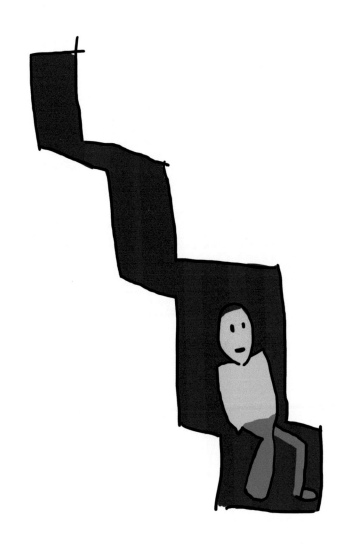

He prepares his backpack and snack.

Then he goes to school.

He listens and follows his teacher.

Lesson of the story:

Every kid must study hard and be responsible so their parents will be happy.

Friday night, he packed his clothes and put them in his luggage.

Saturday morning, he was excited to bring his toys in the car.

Now they're in Vermont! Their room was nice, and his bed was awesome!

He ran, drank water, and ran again! Trees and mountains in Vermont were so high.

They were so hungry. He
wanted pizza and hot dogs!

They went back to the room and slept so tight.

Tomorrow, their vacation is over.

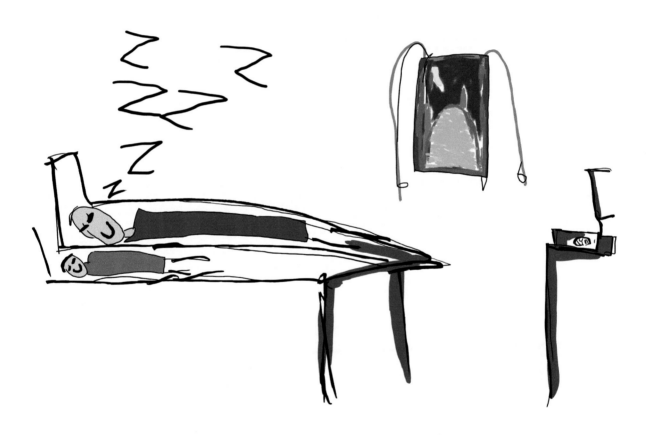

Lesson of the story:

We always go on vacation every time we are free. We are so happy.

The Kid Gets Lost in the Zoo

People go to the zoo, and
they go to see the lions.

Then the kid stays with the lions.

Then the kid can't find his parents.

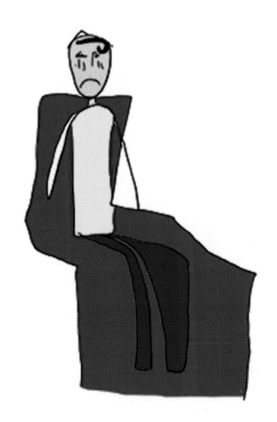

Then the police finds the kid.

The family finds the kid.

Lesson of the story:

Kids, never stay away from your families.

The End

Printed in the United States
By Bookmasters